LEGO

THE LEGO MOVIE

WYLDSTYLE

THE SEARCH FOR THE SPECIAL

WRITTEN BY ANNA HOLMES

Scholastic Children's Books
Euston House,
24 Eversholt Street,
London NW1 1DB, UK

A division of Scholastic Ltd
London - New York - Toronto - Sydney - Auckland
Mexico City - New Delhi - Hong Kong

This book was first published in the US in 2014 by Scholastic Inc.
Published in the UK by Scholastic Ltd, 2014

ISBN 978 1407 15570 8

Based on the Screenplay by PHIL LORD & CHRISTOPHER MILLER
Based on the Story by DAN HAGEMAN & KEVIN HAGEMAN and PHIL LORD & CHRISTOPHER MILLER
Special thanks to Katrine Talks and Matthew Ashton.

Printed and bound by L.E.G.O., Italy

2 4 6 8 10 9 7 5 3 1

SCHOLASTIC

I'm Wyldstyle, and I'm a member of the Master Builders. We're a secret team of super-creative people that can build anything we put our minds to! And we're fighting to stop the evil Lord Business from gluing the world together.

Come with me if you want to hear the story of how I set out to save the world … and wound up finding the only person who could.

According to a prophecy, there was a long-lost "Piece of Resistance" that could defeat Lord Business's super weapon, the Kragle. But no one knew where the Piece of Resistance was hidden. I was determined to find it!

After months of searching, my tracking device led me to a building site in Bricksburg.

DETECTING RELIC

   I suppose I should explain why I wanted to be the
one to find the Piece of Resistance.
   The prophecy said that whoever found it would
be the most important person in the universe. And
I wanted that to be me. I know that sounds super
mature. But for as long as we had been fighting Lord
Business, I couldn't help feeling I was destined to be
"the One."

Suddenly, my tracking device beeped. The Piece of Resistance was nearby! That's when somebody yelled, "Hey, pal, you're not supposed to be here!"

Darn it! I'd been spotted. I was so close to finding the piece!

Luckily, it was just a construction worker and not one of Lord Business's henchmen.

The construction worker chased me and accidently fell into a hole.

Suddenly, Lord Business's police robots showed up, led by Bad Cop!

I expected them to attack, but the robots just passed me by. Instead, they pulled the construction worker out of the rubble. The Piece of Resistance was attached to his back!

I couldn't believe it. After all my searching, *that* guy was the One!

They took the guy away, so I followed them. They chained him up and tried to melt the Piece off of his back. I had to do something!

I fought off the robots ninja-style. Then I grabbed the construction worker, named Emmet, and we escaped on a motorcycle that I quickly built.

Emmet and I raced to the Wild West to find Vitruvius, the leader of the Master Builders. At first, I thought Emmet was pretty cool. After all, he was the Special.

But then I realized something didn't seem right about him. "What's your favourite restaurant?" I asked. "Favourite TV show and song?"

"Any chain restaurant, *Where are My Pants?*, and 'Everything is Awesome!'" he exclaimed.

Oh, no, I thought.

Emmet wasn't special at all! He wasn't even a Master Builder. He was just an ordinary, instruction-following, sitcom-watching, plain-old citizen.

Now I wasn't just disappointed. I was *mad*. "You ruined the prophecy!" I yelled at him. Emmet had taken away the one thing that meant so much to me: the chance to be the Special.

Still, Vitruvius saw something in Emmet that I just couldn't. Then again, Vitruvius is blind.

"The prophecy chose you, Emmet," he said. "All you have to do is believe."

Together, we headed to Cloud Cuckoo Land, a wacky realm where there are no rules whatsoever. All the Master Builders were waiting for us there.

In front of everyone, Emmet tried to give a speech. It didn't go well. The Master Builders could tell that Emmet wasn't cut out to be a leader. They began shouting and throwing things at him!

I felt bad for Emmet. Even though I was disappointed, I didn't want to see him fail. After all, that could have been me up there.

Suddenly, Cloud Cuckoo Land was under attack!
It was Bad Cop again. And this time, he'd brought
hundreds of police robots to the party.

"Go! Run!" I cried. "Everyone, protect the Special!"

Several Master Builders joined us, including UniKitty, a 1980-something spaceman named Benny, and my boyfriend, Batman (did I mention Batman is my boyfriend? It's super serious).

Together, we built a submarine and helped Emmet escape underwater. We had made it out, but the rest of the Master Builders were captured.

The submarine began to flood with water. Luckily, Emmet had built a Double-Decker Couch, and that held together. We all jumped on it and floated to safety. Soon, a Master Builder named Metal Beard picked us up in his pirate ship.

With the other Master Builders taken prisoner by Lord Business, we felt pretty low. How could we stop him from gluing the world together now?

That's when Emmet came up with a plan.

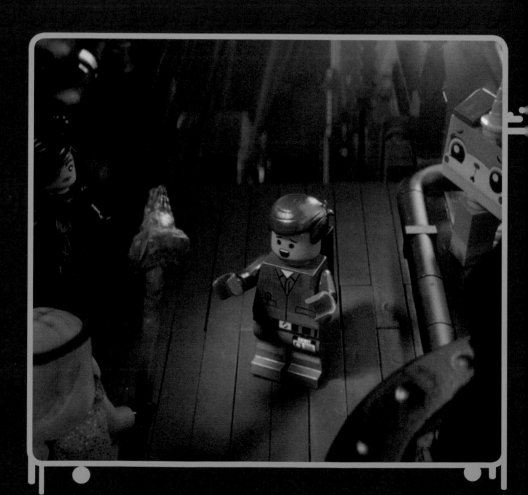

"What's the last thing Lord Business expects us to do?" he said. "Follow the instructions! If we work together, I know we can sneak into Lord Business's tower to stop the Kragle and save the universe!"

For the first time, I saw something different in Emmet. He was acting like a leader. He was acting special.

And I was going to follow him!

Following Emmet's instructions, we built a spaceship just like the ones Lord Business's robots used. Together, we flew up to Lord Business's super-tall office tower.

Emmet and I went to find the Kragle while the others shut off the security.

"I know you put on this tough act, Wyldstyle," Emmet suddenly said to me. "But I don't think that's you. The real you, anyway."

Emmet's kindness made me feel bad about being so tough on him. I decided to tell him the truth. "I wanted it to be me," I admitted. "I wanted to be the Special."

Then, I told Emmet something I'd never told anyone. Not even Batman. "My real name is Lucy. Good luck, Emmet."

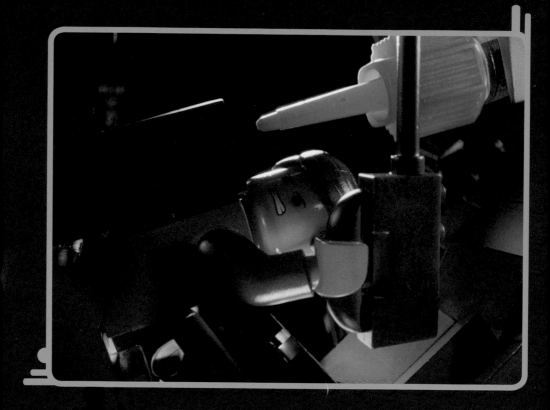

Just as Emmet was about to put the Piece of Resistance on top of the Kragle, Lord Business's robots stormed in. They captured us all!

Lord Business laughed evilly and took the Piece of Resistance off of Emmet's back. Then he threw it out the window!

"Well, I guess there's only one thing left to do," Lord Business said. "Release the Kragle!"

Lord Business strapped Emmet to a battery linked to an explosive device. Then he flew off in his Kraglizer. I looked at Emmet sadly. This couldn't be the end.

Suddenly, Emmet smiled. "It's your turn to be the hero now, Lucy," he said.

Then, he jumped out the window into the infinite abyss!

"No!" I cried.

The wires connecting the battery to the explosive device snapped. We were freed. But Emmet was gone.

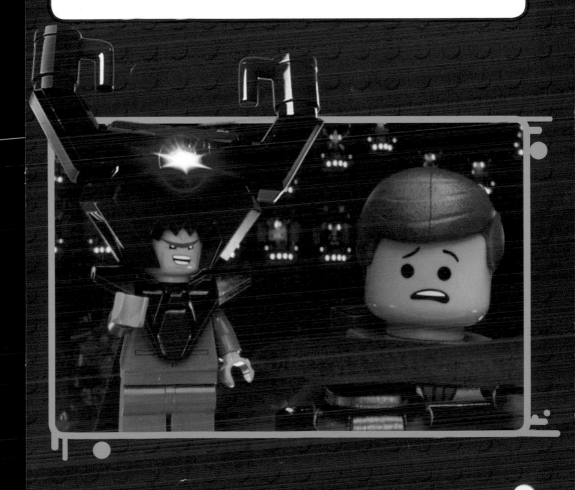

Metal Beard put a hand on my shoulder. "If only there were more people in the world like he."

I looked at the television monitors lining Lord Business's tower. We could see people panicking as Lord Business glued all of Bricksburg together. There were so many people. So many normal citizens ... just like Emmet.

"Maybe there are!" I cried.

Quickly, the Master Builders and I used Lord Business's television cameras to send a message out to the whole universe. I told them about Emmet and how he had saved us.

"Now we have to finish what he started by making whatever weird thing pops into our heads," I said. "We need to fight back against Lord Business."

Together with the people of Bricksburg, we began battling Lord Business's robots. I couldn't believe it. Ice-cream vendors built fighter planes out of their trucks. Bin men turned their dumpsters into chomping spaceships. Everyone was fighting to protect their home. And all because of the inspiration from ...

"Emmet!"

Suddenly, Emmet was back! He was charging through the city in a giant yellow super-machine he had built. And he was carrying the Piece of Resistance!

With the confidence of someone who was truly special, Emmet swung into Lord Business's ship and stopped the Kragle.

I had no idea how he'd done it. But I was too happy to care. Emmet was alive, and he had saved us all!

Emmet had shown me that you didn't need a prophecy or even a Piece of Resistance to be special. You just had to believe in yourself.

And perhaps that was the most special thing of all.